D0382845

The Patient Stone

A Persian Love Story

"The minute I heard my first love story
I started looking for you, not knowing
how blind that was.

Lovers don't finally meet somewhere.
They're in each other all along."
– Rumi

For Jabr Al-Naoimi —
a moth seeking the flame
a drop seeking the sea

And to Tessa and Nancy for contributing
so very much to the ocean of story — M. O. W.

For my mother Carmen, and my wife Ana,
my best critics — J. C. C.

Barefoot Books
37 West 17th Street
4th Floor East
New York, NY 10011

First published in the United States of America in 2001 by Barefoot Books, Inc.

This book was typeset in Veljovic Book 12pt on 21pt leading
The illustrations were prepared in watercolor on paper
Graphic design by designsection, Frome
Color separation by Grafiscan, Italy
Printed and bound in Singapore by Tien Wah Press (Pte) Ltd

This book has been printed on 100% acid-free paper

1 3 5 7 9 8 6 4 2

Library of Congress Cataloging-in-Publication Data:

Wolfson, Margaret, 1953-
The patient stone : a Persian love story / retold by Margaret Olivia
Wolfson : illustrated by Juan Caneba Clavero.
p. cm.
Summary: A retelling of the traditional Persian tale of how the patient
stone helps a mistreated young girl achieve her true destiny.
ISBN 1-84148-085-1
[1. Folklore—Iran. 2. Patience—Folklore.] I. Clavero, Juan Caneba,
ill. II. Title.
PZ8.1 +
398.2'0955'02—dc21

2001000874

THE PATIENT STONE

A Persian Love Story

retold by
Margaret Olivia Wolfson
illustrated by
Juan Cáneba Clavero

Long ago, there lived a girl named Fatima. She was good-natured, kind and trustworthy; she wrote beautiful poetry as well. For these reasons and more, she was loved by all. Still, despite her many admirers, Fatima was often troubled by a strange loneliness.

Now, one day at the village well, Fatima experienced something quite extraordinary. The reflection of a young man's face suddenly rippled across the water's green surface, and a voice whispered, "Fatima, you will soon die."

Fatima whirled around, but saw nothing but a butterfly, its golden wings threaded with sunlight. Facing the well, she again gazed into its depths. To her relief, the face was gone. "I must be imagining things," she told herself.

However, the next day, the same thing happened. This time, Fatima was so alarmed that she turned to her parents for help.

"We must leave here at once!" declared her father.

"And where shall we go?" asked her mother.

"To my brother's village. It's not far. If we hurry, we should be there before nightfall."

So Fatima and her parents packed up some provisions and set out across the desert. They walked and walked, stopping only when the sun sank behind the hills. Fatima's mother cast a worried glance at the barren landscape.

"Are you sure we are going the right way?" she asked her husband anxiously.

"Absolutely," Fatima's father replied. "I've made this trip many times."

"Then perhaps we've been walking too slowly. Let's hope your brother's village lies over the next hill."

But when they reached the top of the hill, all they could see in the desert before them was a walled garden, surrounded on all sides by oceans of moonlit, rippled sand. "We must spend the night there," said Fatima's mother. "It would be unwise to keep traveling in the dark."

And so the three of them wearily made their way to the walled garden. When they arrived, Fatima's father began knocking on its wooden door. Soon, her mother joined in. However, despite their persistent pounding, no one answered. Concluding that the garden's owners were asleep, they decided to enter uninvited. As the door had no handles, they leaned up against it and pushed. Nothing happened.

"Let me try," Fatima said, though she doubted she had strength enough. Miraculously, at her touch, the door swung wide open.

Fatima gazed at the garden before her. A domed dwelling shimmered at its center, and white roses bloomed everywhere, saturating the evening air with their fragrance. The sound of cooing doves echoed through the trees, and dewdrop-jeweled peacocks lay asleep beneath the bushes, their plumage gleaming in the moonlight. A fountain's tumbling waters tinkled like tiny crystal bells. Enchanted, Fatima stepped over the threshold. But no sooner had she done so than the heavy door swung shut behind her.

"Fatima! Fatima!" her parents cried. As if in answer, a strong wind suddenly roared across the desert. Struggling to keep their balance, husband and wife huddled tightly together, only daring to lift their heads when the fierce blowing stopped. It was then that they saw the message in the sand:

If you wish to see your daughter alive, do not enter this garden.
Go home and pray for her freedom.

Sensing great powers at work, Fatima's parents obeyed the mysterious instructions. Silently, they returned to their village.

Inside the garden, Fatima struggled vainly against the closed door. Then she raced all the way around the stone wall, seeking another way out. But there was no sign of another exit anywhere. Fatima turned to look up at the house. Moonlight pearled its domed rooftop, and wide, marble steps flowed up to its entrance like white waves. Convinced that the owners of such a lovely dwelling would be kind-hearted people, Fatima began climbing the stairs. When she reached the top, she pushed open the carved door and stepped inside.

Fatima's eyes widened with wonder at the room before her. Calligraphy danced near the ceiling, and on the walls, mirrors of every shape threw back the light of star-shaped lanterns. Seven doors opened off the room, each painted a different color. Fatima peeked behind the first. There she saw a sunken bath. Its water, lit by candlelight, flashed like golden glass. The second room contained costumes cut from rainbow silks. Fatima tried on several tunics and billowing trousers. All of them fit her perfectly. In the third room, her favorite fruits — apricots, plums, persimmons and pomegranates — were piled high on polished platters. In the fourth room were all sorts of paints, brushes and textured papers. A library greeted her in the fifth, while emeralds, sapphires and diamonds twinkled in the sixth.

However, the seventh room held the greatest surprise of all. Here, a young man slumbered on a low couch. A silken green cloth, embroidered with a golden butterfly, lightly draped his body. A bowl of almonds, a goblet of water and a parchment scroll rested on a nearby table.

Wishing to awaken the youth, Fatima drew back the cover. But when it was halfway off, she stepped back and gasped. Many long pins pierced his heart. For a moment she just stared, too frightened to move. Then the radiance of the young man's glowing face gradually calmed her. As she looked around the room, her eyes fell on the parchment scroll. Quickly, she untied its silken cord, and carefully read its flowing script:

The one lying before you is Javanmard, the Prince of Light. The pins represent faults that cloud the heart. It is your destiny to spend forty nights alone at his side. At the first flush of dawn, you must pluck out a pin. During your vigil, eat and drink little, and do not enter the rooms behind the painted doors. When you remove the fortieth pin, Javanmard will awaken. Success will be yours if you do not succumb to loneliness and doubt.

As she gazed in awe at the prince's radiant face, Fatima vowed to carry out the scroll's instructions. When dusk came, she sat at Javanmard's side, and at the first flush of morning, she removed a pin from his heart. She did the same thing for many dawns until, at last, only one pin remained.

On the thirty-ninth morning, however, such loneliness gnawed at her heart that Fatima found it impossible to rest. She wandered out into the garden, hoping to find the peacocks. It was then that she heard someone singing on the other side of the wall. She hastened back to the house, gathered together an armful of silken sheets and quickly knotted them together. Back outside, she tossed the makeshift rope over the wall.

"Please," she cried out, "I'm dreadfully lonely! I'll reward you for your company!"

The singer — who in truth was a robber girl called Koli — heard Fatima's call. Feeling a bit lonely herself — for she had been traveling for many days without her clan — Koli grasped hold of the rope and climbed up over the wall.

Delighted with her new visitor, Fatima showed her the house and its magical rooms. She even allowed Koli to take a look at Javanmard, explaining that he would awaken when the last pin was plucked from his heart.

Koli's eyes shone. "Why wait?" she said. "Let's take the pin out now!"

Suddenly uneasy, Fatima shut the door. She took a sharp breath and said, "The pins can only be removed at dawn — after a long night's vigil. Besides, I'm the only one who can do it — and I must do it alone."

"Oh then — never mind," Koli said, her pleasant tone in no way revealing the devious plan that was hatching in her mind.

Fatima smiled, grateful her visitor was not offended. "Come," she said, disregarding the scroll's instructions, "let's enjoy the wonderful things behind the painted doors."

And so the girls passed the day, eating the delicious fruit and enjoying the books and paints. But when dusk came, Fatima said, "It's time for me to go to Javanmard."

"Oh Fatima," Koli protested, "don't go, not just yet! We're having such a splendid time! Why, if you stay a little longer, I'll teach you some wonderful songs. You can sing them while you sit by Javanmard. They'll help you pass the time."

And so when Fatima was comfortably settled on a cushion, Koli began to sing. Her melodies were slow and soothing and soon Fatima felt drowsy. Her chin dropped to her chest, and before long, she was fast asleep.

Koli grinned, pleased with the success of her plan. She then hastened to the seventh room, and in one swift movement, plucked the remaining pin from Javanmard's heart. At once, the Prince of Light opened his eyes.

Sitting up, he asked, "Are you the one who freed me?"

"Yes," the wily robber girl lied. "I've been at your side for forty nights."

"And you removed all the pins without any help?"

"Yes," Koli lied again. "The only other person in this house is my servant. And she is forbidden to enter this room."

Javanmard smiled. "Then you are the one destined to be my bride. Will you marry me?"

Just as he uttered these words, Fatima sat bolt upright. She hurried to the seventh room, arriving just in time to see Javanmard and Koli embrace. Sick at heart, Fatima thought, "Because I was not patient enough, I must now suffer the consequences. And though there is nothing I can do now — for why would Javanmard believe me? — I must trust that in time I shall learn how to right this terrible wrong."

So Fatima lived in the house as a servant. When the prince was around, she was treated with kindness, but the moment he turned his back, the proud and overbearing robber girl worked her almost to death. But Fatima never complained — patiently she endured her ordeal.

Now, one day Javanmard announced he was going on a journey. He turned to his wife and asked, "What gift would you like?"

Koli said, "I want an enameled box, engraved with birds and flowers." Javanmard nodded. He then summoned Fatima. "You work long and hard without complaint, so you deserve a gift as well. What shall it be?"

Just then, the voice that she had heard at the well sounded in Fatima's mind. The voice told her to ask for the Patient Stone. Although Fatima had never heard of such a thing, she requested it nonetheless.

Javanmard replied, "I know of no such stone, but I shall do my best to find it."

However, though Javanmard had no trouble finding an enameled box, the Patient Stone proved a mystery. Javanmard was determined to keep his promise, so he followed up on every clue, finding himself in ever darker and more dangerous places. In the end, when he had followed every last lead, he reluctantly gave up his search and set off for home.

The first part of Javanmard's journey went smoothly, but when he reached the halfway point, dark clouds suddenly rolled across the sky and fierce winds whipped the sand into stinging sprays. Seeking shelter, Javanmard retreated into a nearby cave. Much to his surprise, a hermit, all skin and bones and tattered clothes, sat inside. The man's long beard, white as sea spume, foamed into his lap. Firelight flickered in his eyes like a pair of tiny moths.

Thinking the hermit might be hungry, Javanmard offered a sackful of dried fruits. A smile lifted the man's sunken cheeks. "And what can I do for you?" he asked.

Javanmard replied at once, "I'm looking for the Patient Stone. Perhaps you can tell me where to find it."

"And why do you want the Patient Stone?"

"It's not for me," Javanmard explained. "It was requested by my wife's servant girl, Fatima."

The old man looked sharply at Javanmard and said, "That girl is not a servant. She is a pure soul, seeking the garden of truth in a desert of lies. It was her patience, faith and love that drew you from your slumber. But you could not have known this, for you opened your eyes in darkness."

Then the old one waved his hands. As he did so, a pile of slithering, sharp-fanged serpents appeared in the cave. "What you seek rests beneath these snakes," he said. "Fear not, and the Patient Stone will be yours."

Javanmard's stomach churned, but then, remembering his promise to Fatima, he plunged his hand into the cold, hissing heap. At once, he touched something hard and smooth. He curled his fingers around it and drew up the Patient Stone.

The ancient one smiled. "When you get home, hand the stone to Fatima and instruct her to tell it all her sorrows. After you have done this, hide from her sight. But not too far away, for you must be able to hear her speak, and when she falls, to catch her in your arms. Can you do this?"

Solemnly, Javanmard nodded.

When he reached home, the prince found Fatima in the kitchen, polishing silver platters. Javanmard handed her the Patient Stone. "Cradle it in your hands," he said, "and tell it all your sorrows." Then he stepped quietly from the room.

Fatima gazed at the stone. It was dull and grey and rested heavily in her palm. And, although Javanmard's instructions made little sense, she began naming her sorrows.

She spoke of the voice that had prophesied her death and of her journey across the desert. She spoke of the loss of her parents and of the loneliness in her heart. And she spoke of how she had failed Javanmard and of the betrayal and cruelty she had suffered at Koli's hands.

When she had finished, tears pressed against her eyes. Bravely she tried to hold them back, but her long hours of work had drained away her strength and, breaking down, she sobbed in anguish. One by one, her tears dropped onto the Patient Stone.

Suddenly, a crack zigzagged across the rock's surface. In the next moment, the Patient Stone split into two perfect halves. From its core sparkled a fiery light, red and hot as melted rubies. And just as a candle's flame consumes a moth, the heat from the Patient Stone seared Fatima's heart. Drained of life, she shuddered and staggered backwards. At the same moment, Javanmard leapt from behind the curtain and caught her in his arms.

At his touch, life returned to Fatima and she turned to face Javanmard. At first they just gazed at each other, their eyes bright as suns. But then, overcome, they fell into each other's arms and, as they embraced, their hearts and spirits dissolved into one.

The next morning, they set out on the long journey back to Fatima's village. At once, Fatima's parents arranged a great wedding. Fireworks whistled up into the night sky, bejeweling the heavens as they burst open. Fragrant stews, rose-water puddings and honey-drenched cakes were served to all, while sitars, santirs and tambourines rang out in merry measures.

When the celebration finally ended, Fatima and Javanmard returned to their walled garden. And there they lived in happiness and tranquility for many, many years. Needless to say, Fatima was never lonely again, for just as a drop of water finds its home in the sea, her heart had found its home in Javanmard, the shining Prince of Light.

Author's Note

As a children's story, *The Patient Stone* can be enjoyed as a simple tale about the rewards reaped through patience, self-discipline, and courage. However, on an adult level, it is an allegorical story that describes the steps leading to the marriage between soul (Fatima) and spirit (the Prince of Light) — a union symbolically expressed in Sufi literature by the water drop and the sea. Just as a drop of water comes from and returns to the sea, the human soul comes from and returns to its original source — the vast and formless "ocean" of spirit.

To draw out this metaphor I have developed many images associated with water: the prince's reflection is first observed in a well; the garden is surrounded by oceans of sand; dewdrops jewel the peacocks' plumes; marble steps flow upward like white waves; the old man's beard is white as sea spume; the dome of the garden dwelling is pearled with moonlight (pearls are associated with the sea — additionally, in Islamic symbolism, they are believed to hold the most venerable Truth).

I have also encrusted my telling of the story with other imagery and symbolism drawn from mystical Persian literature and lore. These are: the peacock (the closed tail represents the unawakened Self); the ruby (joy and prosperity); the moth (soul seeking the godhead); and the well (symbol of Paradise). The silver platters Fatima is polishing at the story's end represent her heart. In Sufi symbolism the polished heart is likened to a mirror as it both holds and reflects the Divine.

Koli's intrusion into Fatima's world illustrates the Sufi belief that the greatest spiritual opportunities often come in the guise of difficult or painful events. As the Persian mystical poet Jalaluddin Rumi points out: "Wherever there is ruin there is hope for treasure/Why do you not seek the treasure of God in the wasted heart?" And though Sufi doctrine cautions against seeking out calamity, it suggests we bravely face suffering when it comes into our lives. Eventually, Fatima's pain transports her beyond the world of ego (self) and into the world of spirit (Self). Because Fatima did not flee Koli — the personification of darkness — she gains the strength needed to annihilate her loneliness and merge with the Prince of Light.

In many Middle Eastern traditions, the number forty (forty days, forty months, forty years, etc.) is the period of time preceding spiritual transformation.

In addition to enriching the story with Sufi imagery and symbolism, I have expanded the plot — in particular, making the role of the prince more active. In doing so, I sought to express one of the *hadiths* (sayings) attributed to the Prophet Mohammed: "When you take a step towards Him (the Divine), He takes ten steps towards you." The Patient Stone itself might be related to the old Middle Eastern custom of transferring one's sorrow to a stone. In Iranian tradition it is believed that upon hearing of suffering, the Patient Stone bursts open and brings healing to those who confide in it.

Margaret Olivia Wolfson

At Barefoot Books, we celebrate art and story with books that open the hearts and minds of children from all walks of life, inspiring them to read deeper, search further, and explore their own creative gifts. Taking our inspiration from many different cultures, we focus on themes that encourage independence of spirit, enthusiasm for learning, and acceptance of other traditions. Thoughtfully prepared by writers, artists and storytellers from all over the world, our products combine the best of the present with the best of the past to educate our children as the caretakers of tomorrow.

www.barefootbooks.com